The Kingdom of Wrenly

Wrenly

=== 3 ===

Sea Monster!

By Jordan Quinn
Illustrated by Robert McPhillips

LITTLE SIMON
New York London Toronto Sydney New Delhi

LITTLE SIMON
An imprint of Simon & Schuster Children's Publishing Division
1230 Avenue of the Americas, New York, New York 10020
Copyright © 2014 by Simon & Schuster, Inc.
All rights reserved, including the right of reproduction in whole or in part in any form.
LITTLE SIMON is a registered trademark of Simon & Schuster, Inc., and associated colophon is a trademark of Simon & Schuster, Inc.
For information about special discounts for bulk purchases, please contact Simon & Schuster Special Sales at 1-866-506-1949 or business@simonandschuster.com.
The Simon & Schuster Speakers Bureau can bring authors to your live event. For more information or to book an event contact the Simon & Schuster Speakers Bureau at 1-866-248-3049 or visit our website at www.simonspeakers.com.
Manufactured in the United States of America 0116 MTN
6 8 10 9 7 5
Library of Congress Cataloging-in-Publication Data
Quinn, Jordan.
Sea monster! / by Jordan Quinn ; illustrated by Robert McPhillips.
pages cm. — (The kingdom of Wrenly ; 3)
Summary: When a legendary sea monster starts making waves in the Sea of Wrenly, Prince Lucas and his friend Clara travel to the Island of Primlox seeking information that might help them calm the beast.
ISBN 978-1-4814-0072-5 (pbk) — ISBN 978-1-4814-0073-2 (hc) —
ISBN 978-1-4814-0074-9 (eBook) [1. Adventure and adventurers—Fiction.
2. Sea monsters—Fiction. 3. Dragons—Fiction. 4. Princes—Fiction. 5. Friendship—Fiction. 6. Kings, queens, rulers, etc.—Fiction.] I. McPhillips, Robert, illustrator. II. Title.
PZ7.Q31945Se 2014
[E]—dc23
2013020707

CONTENTS

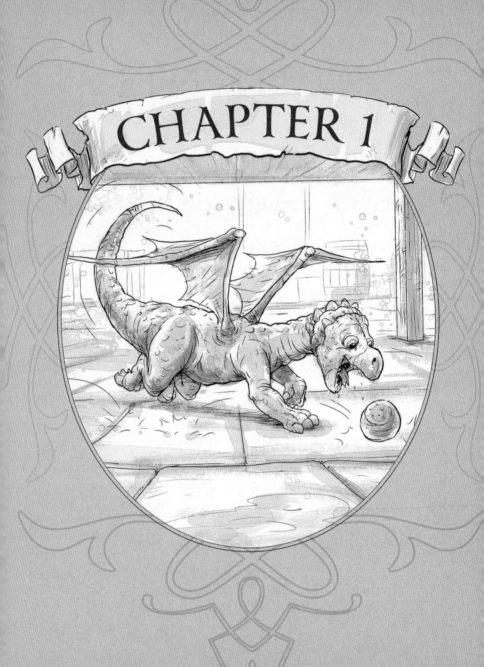

CHAPTER 1

Go Fetch!

Prince Lucas tossed a dinner roll across the royal kitchen. Ruskin, Lucas's pet scarlet dragon, scampered across the stone floor and gobbled the roll in one bite.

"Good boy!" Lucas shouted.

Ruskin ran back to Lucas, eager to fetch another snack. Lucas always sneaked treats for Ruskin when the kitchen servants were on their

afternoon break. He reached for a leftover apple fritter this time.

"The more you eat, the bigger you'll get!" said Lucas.

He couldn't wait for Ruskin to grow big enough to carry him and his best friend, Clara. They dreamed of going on high-flying adventures.

Ruskin yelped for his snack. Lucas threw the apple fritter across the kitchen. The fritter landed next to the hearth. Ruskin zoomed after it, paying no attention to the cast-iron pots and pans stacked neatly beside the hearth. *Crash!* The pots and pans toppled over and clattered across the stone floor.

"What on earth is going on?" bellowed King Caleb, who had just entered the room.

"Oh, not much," said Lucas. "Just getting Ruskin a little snack."

Ruskin burped and a little puff of smoke came out. Lucas waved the smoke away and tried not to laugh.

"Isn't he great?" asked Lucas.

The king raised an eyebrow and polished an apple on his purple velvet robe.

"Tell that to the royal cook," the king said. "Ruskin scorched ten dish towels this week."

Lucas patted Ruskin's swept-back horns.

"He didn't mean any harm," said Lucas.

"Nevertheless," said the king, "he'll need better manners if he's going to come inside the castle."

Lucas had been training Ruskin to be a good dragon. The problem was that Ruskin didn't know how to control his fire-breathing. Sometimes he had accidents, and sometimes he scorched things for fun. Lucas was trying to teach Ruskin to use his fire-breathing skills for good causes, like lighting the hearth or roasting marshmallows.

"Don't worry, Father," said Lucas. "Soon Ruskin will be the most well-behaved dragon in all of Wrenly."

"Well, that's the best news I've heard all day," said the king as he left the room, munching his apple.

CHAPTER 2

A Creature from the Sea

Lucas and Ruskin played one more game of fetch the snack. Then Lucas stuffed an apple fritter into his pocket for later. The two playmates skipped past King Caleb on their way outside. The king sat on his throne and stared out to sea.

Lucas turned around.

"Is something wrong, Father?" Lucas asked.

The king scrunched his brow and sighed.

"Perhaps," he said. "We've had some troubling reports from the fishermen."

"About what?" asked Lucas.

"Giant waves in and around the Sea of Wrenly," the king said.

"Must be a storm brewing," Lucas said.

"That's my guess," said the king, "but some say they've seen a large creature in the water."

"What kind of creature?" asked Lucas, becoming more interested.

"Something big," the king said. "Like a whale or a giant octopus."

"Or maybe a sea monster!" said Lucas.

The king raised an eyebrow. "That's ridiculous!" he said. "There are no such things as sea monsters."

Ruskin squawked.

"That's not what I've heard," Lucas said. "My old nursemaid, Nanny Louisa, told me a story about a sea monster. She said she saw it with her own eyes."

The king chuckled. "I know that story too," he said. "The legend of the

Great Sea Serpent has been around for years."

"It has?" questioned Lucas.

The king nodded.

"But how do you know it's not true?"

"Because it's not," said the king. "And I certainly don't want my people to worry about something that doesn't exist."

Ruskin let out a long, low howl.

Lucas and the king looked at the young dragon.

"Good heavens," commented the king. "What do you suppose he is trying to say?"

"I don't know," said Lucas. "Maybe that he believes in sea serpents."

CHAPTER 3

An Old Wives' Tale

"Well, I believe in sea monsters too!" said Lucas. "And I have a plan."

Ruskin scampered after Lucas. They ran all the way to Ruskin's lair. Once they were inside, Lucas played a trick on Ruskin. He reached into his pocket, pulled out the apple fritter, and tossed it deep into the cave. Ruskin ran after it. Then Lucas turned around and ran back out

the entrance. He slid the heavy oak
door across the opening and locked
Ruskin inside. Ruskin whimpered.

"Sorry, boy," Lucas said. "But this
plan doesn't include you. It may get
dangerous."

Ruskin squawked loudly.

"Someday, when you're bigger and stronger, you can come with me," said Lucas. "But not this time."

Lucas raced back to the castle
and into the chambers belonging to
his mother, Queen Tasha. He opened
the door and bumped into Anna
Gills. A few bolts of fabric fell from

her arms. Anna was the royal seamstress. She was also Clara's mother.

"I'm so sorry, ma'am," said Lucas
as he helped pick up the fabric.

"What's the hurry, Lucas?" asked
Anna.

"Forgive me for rushing," said
Lucas. "I'm looking for Clara. Do
you know where I can find her?"

Anna smiled.

"Clara is at Mermaid's Cove, collecting seashells," she said.

Lucas thanked Anna and zoomed off. He jumped from rock to rock as he bounded down the path to the beach. Something scrabbled over the

rocks behind him. Lucas stopped and turned around. He didn't see anything. *I thought I heard something behind me,* he wondered to himself. *I guess I must have kicked a rock.*

Lucas continued down the path. He spotted Clara sitting on a large rock. Her brown hair was partly up in a braided crown. She held a string of shells in her hand. An old net lay on the rock behind her.

"What's that?" asked Lucas, stopping in the sand in front of Clara.

"It's an old fishing net," Clara said. "It washed up on the beach today. It's perfect for stringing shells."

Clara held out a necklace. It had

slipper shells, moon shells, and angel wings.

"It's beautiful," said Lucas as he hopped up and sat on the rock beside his friend. "So, you'll never guess what!"

"What?" asked Clara.

"There's a monster lurking in the Sea of Wrenly," Lucas said.

Clara's eyes widened. "What makes you say that?" she asked.

"My father says some of the

fishermen have seen a huge creature in the water. I'm pretty sure it's the Great Sea Serpent."

Clara laughed. "That's silly. Everyone knows that the sea serpent story is just an old wives' tale."

"I'm not so sure," said Lucas.

"Do you actually believe in sea monsters?"

"Yes, I really do," said Lucas. "My old nursemaid, Nanny Louisa, told me she saw the Great Sea Serpent with her own eyes."

"She did?" questioned Clara.

Lucas nodded. "And she would never make up something like that," he added.

"I never dreamed that story could be true," said Clara. "What do you think we should do?"

"Let's talk to Nanny Louisa," said Lucas. "Maybe she can help."

"Where does she live?" asked Clara.

"On the island of Primlox," said Lucas. "She's now a nurse to the fairies."

Clara slipped her shell necklace into her leather pouch. "What are we waiting for?" she asked. "Let's go!"

CHAPTER 4

Nanny Louisa

Lucas and Clara ran to the royal stables to saddle their horses, Ivan and Scallop.

Lucas lifted a saddle from the wooden saddle rack. Something in the window above him caught his attention. He climbed onto the saddle rack and peeked outside.

"What are you looking at?" Clara asked.

"I saw something in the window,"
Lucas said. "But now there's nothing
out there."

"Maybe it was a bird," said Clara.

Lucas shrugged. "Maybe," he said.

Lucas and Clara placed a saddle
onto each horse and tightened the
straps. Then they set off for Primlox.

As they galloped past Flatfrost, Lucas noticed whitecaps on the water up ahead. *Wow, the sea monster really is making the water choppy,* Lucas thought.

When they got near the bridge,
they pulled back on their reins.
Villagers rushed back and forth
across the bridge.

"The bridge sure is busy," Clara said.

"We'll have to walk the horses over it," said Lucas.

They led Ivan and Scallop over the bridge and tied them to a post on the other side. The harbormaster

stood nearby, ringing his hands.

"What's wrong?" Lucas asked.

"It's been a very bad day, Prince Lucas," said the harbormaster. "The sea is too rough for travelers." He walked up closer and leaned in toward Lucas. "And there have been

rumors of something in the ocean."

Lucas and Clara gave each other a knowing glance.

"Well, we've come to see Nanny Louisa," said Lucas. "Do you know where she might be?"

The harbormaster nodded. "She's

tending to Fairy Queen Sophie. The queen has a very bad cold."

Lucas and Clara thanked him and headed for the fairy castle, a beautiful palace made of polished pebbles, shells, and sea glass. The fairies-in-waiting led them up the

curvy stone staircase to Queen Sophie's chambers.

"*Ah-choo!*" The queen sneezed as the guests entered the room.

A puff of sparkly fairy dust flew from Queen Sophie's nose and mouth. She was sitting in her canopy bed, wearing a pink silk nightgown with enchanted milkweed fluff around the neck.

Nanny Louisa sat in a rocking chair beside Queen Sophie's bed. She handed her a handkerchief. Then Nanny Louisa stood up and greeted their guests. "Well, if it isn't my

chubby little bunny and his friend!"

Lucas blushed and Clara giggled. Lucas had been a very chubby baby, and Nanny Louisa always brought it up. She held out her jiggly arms and gave Lucas a great big hug. Then she looked at Clara.

"I remember you," said Nanny Louisa. "You deliver bread with your father. And your mother is Queen Tasha's seamstress."

Clara recognized Nanny Louisa too. She had a round, dwarflike body

and long white hair. Her eyes were
kind and her smile was wide. Lucas
formally introduced the two.

"Please excuse my stuffy nose,"
said Queen Sophie. "Tell me: What

brings you to the palace?"

Nanny Louisa pulled up two chairs, and Lucas and Clara sat down.

"We have some questions for Nanny Louisa," said Lucas.

"We also wondered if you've heard the rumors," Clara said.

"What rumors?" asked Nanny Louisa.

Queen Sophie sat up in bed. "Yes, what rumors?" she asked.

"The Sea of Wrenly has been unusually rough," Lucas said, "and some say they've seen a big creature in the water."

Nanny Louisa's eyes grew wide, and she placed one hand over her mouth. "Oh no," she whispered. "The Great Sea Serpent."

Lucas nodded.

"You're joking, right?" questioned Queen Sophie.

But nobody laughed.

"Tell us, Nanny Louisa," said Lucas. "Is the sea serpent real—or not?"

Nanny Louisa sank into her rocking chair and sighed. "Most believe the sea serpent to be a myth," she said. "But those who have seen the great beast feel differently."

"We would love to hear your story, Nanny Louisa," said Clara.

"Yes, please tell it!" begged Lucas.

Nanny Louisa shut her eyes and told the story from long ago.

CHAPTER 5

Once in a Blue Moon

"I remember the day well," Nanny Louisa began. "I was a young maiden in those days—not a single gray hair nor a wrinkle. I worked at the Dew Drop Inn. I often served a young gentleman known as Captain Douglas Brown. Captain Brown was strong, kind, and well-liked in the village. One rainy night he asked me to be the cook aboard his ship, the

Blue Moon. He planned to take some men on a fishing trip. I have always liked adventure, so I agreed to go.

"We sailed the open sea for three weeks. The boys caught mackerel, tuna, and herring. Then we set our course for home. I stood on deck and

enjoyed a gentle breeze. I watched the clouds turn pink. Then my eyes fell on a dark patch of water. *A patch of seaweed,* I thought to myself. I looked more closely and noticed the dark water begin to boil and churn. *A pod of dolphins?* I wondered.

"Then something unimaginable happened. A creature began to rise from the water. It rose higher and higher—above and beyond the mast of the *Blue Moon*. It had the head of a dragon, with two horns and a mouth full of daggerlike teeth. The creature had a never-ending neck of green scales for a body, like an enormous snake.

"But the strangest thing of all was the rusty old cauldron that hung from the monster's jaw. It looked like a wizard's cauldron, though cracked and broken. *Why*

does it have a cauldron in its mouth?
I wondered.

"I stared—too scared to move. A brave sailor grabbed a spyglass and climbed the rigging to the crow's nest to get a better look. Others began to throw things at the creature: boat hooks, silverware, and

dishes—anything that might scare it away. The monster roared and threw his head to one side. Then it flung the cauldron right at our ship!

"The cauldron crashed onto the deck, and we dove to get out of its path. The ship rocked this way and that. Captain Brown quickly spun the wheel to get us to safety. Then the men pulled themselves up and threw more things at the monster."

Nanny Louisa shut her eyes and rocked in the chair as she remembered the story.

"Please go on, Nanny Louisa!" cried Lucas.

"Oh yes!" exclaimed Clara. "Tell us what happened next!"

Nanny Louisa opened her eyes and continued her story.

CHAPTER 6

A Message

"'Wait! Leave the beast alone!'
Captain Brown shouted.

"The fishermen stopped striking
the sea monster. The serpent roared
and plunged beneath the water.
Enormous waves rocked our ship.
Green seawater splashed over the
deck. *We're done for!* I thought as
I landed on top of my shipmates.
Somehow I dragged myself to my

feet and looked out on the water.

"The sea serpent slithered away. Loop after loop of its scaly green body curled through the water as it went on its way. None of us spoke.

We looked at the cauldron, which had left a large hole in the deck. *Had the monster been trying to tell us something?* we wondered. Perhaps the monster didn't like that garbage was being thrown into its watery home. We all agreed that the people of Wrenly needed to change their ways.

"Captain Brown took us to port.

We told King Henry—King Caleb's father—what we had seen and heard. The king believed every word of our story. He knew he could trust Captain Brown.

"'But you must never speak of it,' said the king. 'We mustn't upset the good people of Wrenly.' He also said that if we didn't have evidence of a monster, then no one would believe our tale. Then King Henry made a royal decree:

HEAR YE! HEAR YE!

BY ROYAL DECREE OF THE KING OF WRENLY:

NO DUMPING GARBAGE INTO THE SEA!

LAWBREAKERS WILL BE THROWN IN THE DUNGEON FOR TEN DAYS.

"Some of the fishermen told the story of the sea serpent against the king's wishes. But no one believed them. The villagers made fun of the fishermen and called them crazy. But I'm here to say—cross my heart— that every word of this story is true."

Everyone sat in silence.

Then Lucas said, "I believe you, Nanny Louisa. I've always believed you."

"I believe you too," said Clara.

"And I," said Queen Sophie.

"But what do we do now?" Lucas asked.

CHAPTER 7

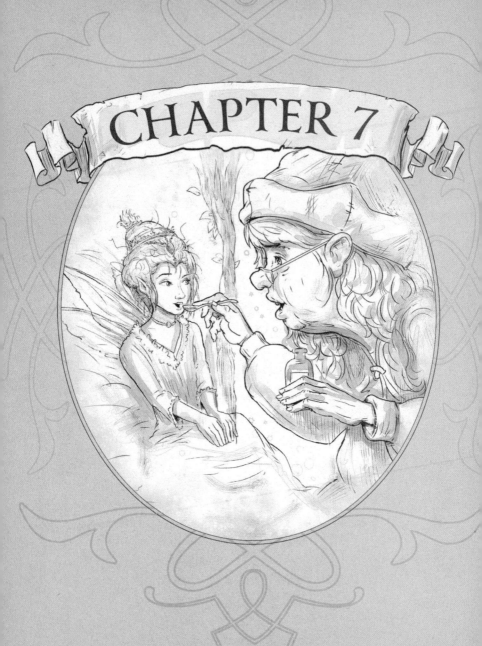

Captain Brown

"Here's what you must do," said Nanny Louisa as she gave a doll-size spoonful of a potion to Queen Sophie. "You must find out what's bothering the sea serpent."

"But how?" asked Clara.

"There's only one way," said Nanny Louisa. "You must find the sea serpent and let him tell you."

Lucas and Clara looked at each

other and gulped. But Nanny Louisa was right. How else could they find out what was bothering the sea serpent?

"We're up to the task!" said Lucas and Clara together.

"Will you come with us, Nanny Louisa?" asked Clara.

"No," said Nanny Louisa. "I must stay with Queen Sophie until she feels better."

Queen Sophie had fallen asleep while they were talking.

"Then we'll be on our way," Lucas said. "Thank you for everything, Nanny Louisa."

Nanny Louisa hugged Lucas and Clara. "Be careful," she said.

"We will," promised Lucas.

Lucas and Clara hurried down the hill to the water. Empty ships bobbed up and down at the dock. Lucas tapped the harbormaster on the shoulder.

"We need a ship," Lucas said.

The harbormaster turned and faced Lucas and Clara.

"I'm sorry, Prince Lucas," he said. "But the captains have all gone home for the day.

Nobody wants to

set sail in this rough water."

"But we're here on official royal
business," said Lucas in his most
grown-up voice. "We need to search
for the sea monster."

The harbormaster stroked his
chin thoughtfully. He knew better
than to argue with royalty.

"Excuse me," said a scruffy-looking man who had been listening in. "May I be of some help?"

The man had a toothless smile, like a jack-o'-lantern's. He wore a tattered brown coat and old trousers. His knotted gray beard matched his straggly gray hair. He face was weathered, and he had friendly blue eyes.

"Who are you?" Lucas asked.

"I'm Captain Brown," said the man.

Clara and Lucas gasped.

"*The* Captain Douglas Brown?" asked Lucas.

"At your service," said the captain.

"But how did you find us?" asked Clara.

"A special friend sent for me," said Captain Brown. "She said it was urgent."

"Nanny Louisa!" cried Lucas.

"Aye. She may have had a bit of a part in it," the captain said.

"I'm not sure I like the idea of the

prince and a young maiden hunting for sea monsters," interrupted the harbormaster.

"Come," said Captain Brown, ignoring the harbormaster. "My ship, the *Blue Moon*, awaits. Have you any payment?"

Lucas and Clara looked at each other. They didn't have a single shilling. Then Clara reached into her pocket and pulled out her shell necklace.

Captain Brown smiled. "That will do nicely," he said. "Let's go find ourselves a sea monster."

Then they followed the toothless, bearded captain to his ship.

CHAPTER 8

An Old Friend

The ship pulled away from the dock and suddenly leaned to the right. Lucas and Clara held on to the side of the ship to keep from tumbling into the water.

"How are we going to find the sea monster?" asked Clara.

"Don't worry," said Captain Brown. "The sea serpent is going to find *us*."

"What could be bothering him?" Lucas asked.

"We shall soon find out," said the captain.

Sailing around the mainland, they passed Hobsgrove, Crestwood, and Burth. Saltwater sprayed as they rode up and down the waves. Lucas thought he saw something flicker in the crow's nest. He looked closely but didn't see anything. *My eyes must be playing tricks on me,* he thought.

When Primlox came back into view, they had seen no sign of the sea monster.

"Where is that old beast?" the captain shouted over the wind.

"Let's go around again!" yelled Lucas.

"It's too rough!" said Captain Brown. "We'll try again tomorrow."

"Please!" begged Lucas. "Just one more time around!"

Before Captain Brown could answer, the ship began to rock violently.

The ocean rumbled like thunder. The water churned and boiled, like a bubbling broth.

"Hold on!" Captain Brown shouted.

Clara and Lucas clutched the side of the ship with all their strength.

"What's happening?" Lucas cried.

"It's my old friend!" shouted Captain Brown as he pointed to the water up ahead. "The sea monster!"

Lucas and Clara saw the beast rise out of the water. They both screamed. It had the head of a fearsome dragon and a neck that

stretched on forever—just as Nanny Louisa had described! Its green scales shimmered in the gray afternoon light.

The ship
jerked violently this
way and that. Lucas lost his grip
and tumbled across the deck.
He managed to grab hold of a rope
to keep from falling into the water.
When he looked up, the sea monster towered over the ship. It roared.
Then it lunged right at them.

Captain Brown spun the wheel away from the sea monster, but the captain lost control of the boat. Seawater flooded the deck.

"Hang on!" the captain cried.

CHAPTER 9

A Swirl of Fire

Somehow the ship stayed afloat. But the sea monster roared with fury. *It's going to swallow us whole!* Lucas thought. He squeezed his eyes shut.

"Lucas, open your eyes!" shouted Clara. "I see something caught on the sea monster's head!"

"She's right!" Captain Brown shouted.

Lucas opened his eyes and looked.

He hadn't seen it before, but the sea monster had a net stuck on its head.

"How can we free it?" asked Clara.

"We need to get closer!" shouted Lucas.

"Too dangerous!" cried Captain Brown.

Squawk! cried something from the crow's nest.

"What was that?" shouted Lucas.

"Up there!" yelled Clara.

A streak of red flew from the crow's nest.

"It's Ruskin!" Lucas yelled.

Ruskin squawked again and flew onto the sea monster's head. The sea monster tried to shake him off. But

Ruskin clung on to him.

"What's he doing?" Captain Brown shouted.

"I think he's trying to free the sea monster!" said Lucas.

Ruskin pulled at the net on the sea monster's head. He tugged and tugged, but the net wouldn't come free. Suddenly, Ruskin roared, and a little swirl of flame burned away some of the netting. Then Ruskin easily removed the rest of the net and flew a short distance away.

The sea monster shook its head. Its face became calm, and it sank

back into the sea. The water stopped churning, and the boat stopped jerking this way and that. Ruskin flew back to the ship and landed on the deck. He dropped the net at Lucas's feet.

Clara leaned over and picked it up.

"It's an old fishing net!" she exclaimed. "Just like the ones I use

to string my shell necklaces."

"The fishermen must be tossing their old nets into the sea," said Lucas. "And this one got tangled around the sea monster's head."

"No wonder the sea monster was mad!" said Captain Brown.

"Wow," said Clara. "If it hadn't been for Ruskin, the sea monster would have sunk our ship."

"Good boy, Ruskin," said Lucas, patting him on the back. "You used your fire to do something good!"

Ruskin rubbed his head against Lucas's legs.

"How do you think Ruskin found us?" asked Clara.

"I'm not sure," Lucas said. "I must've left the escape exit open, and then he was able to follow us by flying high above."

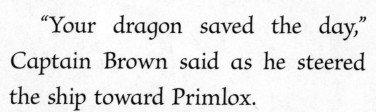

"Your dragon saved the day," Captain Brown said as he steered the ship toward Primlox.

Ruskin squawked.

"He sure did," Lucas said.

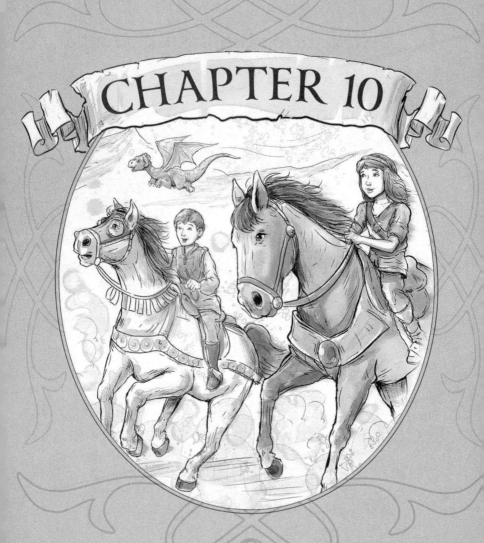

CHAPTER 10

A Royal Decree

The ship docked at Primlox, and Lucas and Clara said good-bye to their new friend, Captain Brown. They unhitched Ivan and Scallop and galloped back to the palace. Ruskin flew close behind.

The sun had gone down by the time they reached the stables. The stable hand began to feed and water their horses. Lucas and Clara thanked him and raced to the great hall with Ruskin at their heels. The king, the queen, and Anna jumped up from the table when the children walked in.

"Where on earth have you been?" demanded King Caleb.

"We were so worried!" said Queen Tasha.

"Just look at you two!" said Anna.

Lucas and Clara looked like they'd been washed in with the tide. Their clothes were soaked, and they had seaweed tangled in their hair.

"We went looking for the sea monster," said Lucas.

The king raised his hands and looked at the ceiling. "And did you find one?" he asked.

Lucas and Clara looked at each other and grinned. Then they shared their adventure.

"And Ruskin freed the sea monster with a little swirl of fire," finished Lucas.

Clara pulled the fishing net from her pouch and placed it on the table. The queen and Anna looked it over.

"Quite a remarkable tale," said the king. "You two certainly have wild imaginations."

Then Queen Tasha put a hand on the king's shoulder. "I'm not sure they're making it up," she said. "Look at this."

Caught in the net was a shimmering green scale. The king untangled it and looked at it closely. He turned it over and rubbed it between his fingers.

"Well, look at that," said the king.

"*Now* do you believe us?" asked Lucas.

"Yes," said the king. "I'm afraid I do."

Lucas folded his arms. "There's one thing I don't get."

"What's that?" asked the king.

"How come people get scared when they hear rumors of a sea serpent? And then, if someone actually finds one, they don't believe it?"

"Well," said the king, "sometimes you have to see something in order to believe it."

"Like you?" Lucas asked.

"Yes," said the king. "Like me."

"Are you going to tell the people of Wrenly that the sea serpent is real?" asked Lucas.

"Yes," said the king as he laid the scale on the table. "Since we have proof, I will tell the people, and I will also make a new decree. I shall call it the Rule of the Great Sea Serpent.

From now on, no fishing nets shall be thrown into the Sea of Wrenly. They must be mended or thrown away properly. Lawbreakers will be sent to the dungeon for ten days."

Then Lucas made his own royal decree. "Hear ye! Hear ye!" he said in loud voice. "I hereby proclaim that I am as hungry as a sea monster!"

"Me too!" Clara chimed in.

Everyone sat at

the table—except for Ruskin, who sat on the floor beside Lucas's chair— and had a dinner of pork roast, vegetables, and Ruskin's favorite: apple fritters. Ruskin ate five apple fritters and burped. A little ball of fire slipped out and charred the tablecloth.

Everyone laughed—even the king.

Hear ye! Hear ye!
Presenting the next book from
The Kingdom of Wrenly!
Here's a sneak peek!

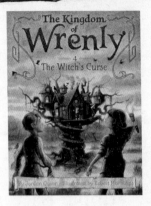

Stefan presented the Witch of Bogburp to the king and queen.

Ruskin took one look at the witch and scampered behind Lucas. Lucas remembered her slightly from when she had worked at the palace.

The witch had a short, stubby body, a large hooked nose, and elf-ish ears. She wore a black cloak, and wet pointy leather shoes on her feet.

Excerpt from *The Witch's Curse*

A bonnet with a tail and a tassel sat on top of her scraggly black hair, and where her left eye should have been, the witch had a glass eye. To top it off, she had a black raven perched on top of her walking stick.

"What brings you to the castle, Tilda?" asked the king in a calm but not-so-friendly tone.

The Witch of Bogburp smiled, revealing a missing tooth on one side. She bowed slightly. "I have come to mend my ways, Your Majesty."

"And how do you plan to mend your ways?" asked the king.

Excerpt from *The Witch's Curse*

A crooked smile swept over the witch's face as lightning flashed outside the throne room windows.

"Why, I can put an end to all this rain," she said sweetly.

Thunder boomed and rumbled around the castle.

King Caleb looked at the witch suspiciously. "And what do you know about the rain?" he asked.

"I know it's a curse," said the witch.

The king leaned back in his throne. "And what do you want to do about it?" he asked.

Excerpt from *The Witch's Curse*

The witch's glass eye bulged in its socket. "I don't *want* to do anything," she said. "I like the rain. But if never-ending rain isn't good for your kingdom, I may be able to help."

The king desperately needed help. He had no idea how to stop the rain, and the witch knew it. He couldn't allow all the crops to be ruined.

"I suppose I will have to accept your offer," said the king.

"Of course you will," said the witch, who now knew that she, not the king, had the power. "But there will be a small price to pay."

Excerpt from *The Witch's Curse*